PRINCE OF PERSIA

BEFORE THE SANDSTORM

By
JORDAN MECHNER

ART BY
TOM FOWLER, DAVID LOPEZ,
BERNARD CHANG, TOMMY LEE EDWARDS,
CAMERON STEWART, NIKO HENRICHON,
PETE PANTAZIS, AND DAVE STEWART

LETTERING BY
ROB LEIGH AND JOHN WORKMAN

BASED ON THE SCREENPLAY WRITTEN BY

DOUG MIRO & CARLO BERNARD

FROM A SCREEN STORY BY
JORDAN MECHNER AND BOAZ YAKIN

EXECUTIVE PRODUCERS
MIKE STENSON, CHAD OMAN, JOHN AUGUST,
JORDAN MECHNER, PATRICK McCORMICK, ERIC McLEOD

PRODUCED BY
JERRY BRUCKHEIMER

DIRECTED BY
MIKE NEWELL

DISNEP PRESS
New York

YOU WOULD HAVE DONE BETTER TO RETURN HOME TO YOUR WIFE AND CHILDREN. A MAN WHO CONSORTS WITH CRIMINALS IS AS GUILTY AS THEY.

THE MERCHANTS TOLD US THAT THE ITEMS HAD BEEN PAID FOR WITH COINS AND TRINKETS OF EVERY DESCRIPTION, WHICH THESE MEN CARRIED IN A LARGE SACK.

THIS IS WHAT WAS LEFT. THE GUARDS FOUND IT HIDDEN IN THE HOUSE.

"HIDDEN..." BAH!

THIS BRACELET CARRIES THE INSIGNIA OF KING SHARAMAN HIMSELF. IT BELONGS TO THE ROYAL FAMILY.

EXACTLY! THE ROYAL FAMILY. GOVERNOR, ALLOW ME TO EXPLAIN.

I WAS MINDING MY OWN BUSINESS, WITH MY GOOD FRIEND SESO HERE...TOILING IN THE SALT MINES, AN HONEST DAY'S WORK FOR A DAY'S PAY...

SHEIKH AMAR! HORSEMEN COMING.

PERSIANS. COULD THEY BE...DO YOU THINK...

TAX COLLECTORS?

HIDE EVERYTHING! THE GOATS, THE OSTRICHES... DEAR GOD, WE HAVE A RACE TOMORROW. THEIR TIMING COULDN'T BE WORSE.

NO ONE FINDS THIS PLACE BY ACCIDENT. SOMEONE MUST HAVE TALKED.

ACT INNOCENT. IF WE'RE LUCKY, THEY WON'T LOOK IN THE TUNNELS.

THE KING'S MEN RODE UP OUT OF THE DESERT. WHICH WAS UNUSUAL, THE SALT MINES BEING SOMEWHAT OUT OF THE WAY, BUT WELCOME NONETHELESS.

NATURALLY, I GREETED THEM, AND INQUIRED HOW I MIGHT BE OF SERVICE.

DO YOU KNOW A SHEIKH AMAR?

THAT DEPENDS.

MAY I ASK WHY YOU'RE LOOKING FOR HIM?

PRINCE DASTAN WISHES TO REWARD SHEIKH AMAR AND AN AFRICAN CALLED "SESO" FOR THEIR SERVICE TO THE REALM.

WHO IS PRINCE DASTAN?

DON'T ASK ME.

...THEY LEFT THE TREASURE AND RODE OFF. THAT'S THE TRUTH. I SWEAR ON MY OWN MOTHER-- MAY SHE SUFFER THE PANGS OF ETERNAL CONSTIPATION IF I'M LYING.

I THOUGHT TO MYSELF, WHAT WOULD I, A SIMPLE MAN OF THE DESERT, DO WITH SUCH TREASURE? MY NEEDS ARE FEW.

BUT I AM A RIVER TO MY PEOPLE. AND SO I DECIDED TO THROW A BANQUET TO SHARE MY GOOD FORTUNE.

DO YOU EXPECT US TO BELIEVE THAT PRINCE DASTAN WOULD REWARD A PAIR OF ROGUES LIKE YOU-- STRANGERS HE'S NEVER EVEN MET--WITH SUCH WEALTH? REWARD YOU FOR *WHAT*?

IF I WERE LYING, YOU CAN BE SURE I'D INVENT A MORE CONVINCING STORY.

BUT THAT'S JUST IT. I DON'T KNOW. WHICH *PROVES* I'M TELLING THE TRUTH.

AS THE POET SAID: "A THIEF IS A KING UNTIL HE'S CAUGHT."

I'VE HEARD ENOUGH. HAVE THE OTHER THREE FLOGGED AND THESE TWO BEHEADED. INFORM THE ROYAL PALACE THAT WE ARE HOLDING THEIR PROPERTY.

ON MY WAY, SIR!

WAIT! WAIT! WAIT! IT JUST OCCURRED TO ME... OF COURSE! WHAT A FOOL I AM--WHY DIDN'T I THINK OF IT BEFORE?

YOUR POINT?

PRINCE DASTAN...KING SHARAMAN'S YOUNGEST SON, YES? THE ONE HE ADOPTED AND RAISED AS HIS OWN? (WHICH GOES TO SHOW WHAT A GOOD AND GENEROUS KING HE IS...MAY HE LIVE TEN THOUSAND YEARS... AND MAY HIS GOVERNORS AND TAX COLLECTORS LIVE TEN THOUSAND YEARS...)

PRINCE DASTAN-- I *HAVE* MET HIM! IT'S JUST THAT HE WASN'T YET A PRINCE.

IN MY YOUTH I TRAVELED A GREAT DEAL--A KEY FOR ANY BUSINESSMAN WHO HOPES TO SUCCEED IN TODAY'S PERSIA.

MY TRAVELS BROUGHT ME TO THE CITY OF **SIRAF**... WHERE AN UNFORTUNATE MISUNDERSTANDING--SIMILAR IN CERTAIN RESPECTS TO THE ONE WE'RE EXPERIENCING TODAY--LED TO MY ARREST AND TEMPORARY INCARCERATION IN THE DUNGEONS OF **KING SHARAMAN,** MAY HE LIVE TWENTY THOUSAND YEARS.

SHEIKH AMAR'S TALE
Art by Bernard Chang

YOU SEE, EXCELLENCY, I'M HIDING NOTHING FROM YOU. A MAN IN MY SITUATION COULD EASILY POLISH UP HIS RÉSUMÉ A BIT TO PRESENT HIMSELF IN A MORE FLATTERING LIGHT.

BUT I, AS AN HONEST MAN WITH NOTHING TO HIDE, I TELL YOU WITHOUT SHAME THAT I'VE BEEN IN PRISON.

THIS IS A MISTAKE! I CAN EXPLAIN!

ONE DAY, AS I WAITED PATIENTLY FOR THE AUDIENCE WITH THE GOVERNOR THAT WOULD CLEAR THINGS UP, THE GUARDS WERE KIND ENOUGH TO RELIEVE MY SOLITUDE BY BRINGING ME A ROOMMATE.

A *TWO-LEGGED* ROOMMATE.

I'M A POOR MAN. NOT WORTH ROBBING.

I'M NOT A THIEF.

A *MURDERER,* THEN?

HE WAS A YOUNG PERSIAN, MODEST IN DEMEANOR AND APPEARANCE. I LIKED HIM IMMEDIATELY.

MY ONLY CRIME WAS TO FALL IN LOVE WITH A WOMAN I CAN NEVER HAVE.

SAME HERE! ONLY IN MY CASE, IT WAS AN OSTRICH.

THAT CAME OUT WRONG. WHAT I MEAN TO SAY IS, WE'RE BOTH INNOCENT.

I'VE GOT TO FIND A WAY OUT OF HERE. SHE CAN'T MARRY HIM--IT WOULD BE MONSTROUS.

MARRY WHO?

THE GRAND VIZIER. *JAFFAR.*

FOR AN HOUR HE RAN AND CLIMBED AND TESTED EVERY STONE IN THAT CELL UNTIL HE FINALLY GAVE UP. I'VE NEVER SEEN ANYONE SO TIRELESS.

EVENTUALLY HE SETTLED DOWN AND BEGAN TO TELL ME HIS STORY.

I WAS STRUCK ONCE AGAIN BY ITS PARALLELS TO MY OWN.

SHE'S A PRINCESS.

THE MOST PERFECT, BEAUTIFUL CREATURE I'VE EVER SEEN. AND I'M NOBODY, FROM NOWHERE.

IT WAS MONTHS AGO. I HAD GONE TO THE MARKET TO PICK UP SOME FOOD.

STOP HIM, IN THE NAME OF KING SHARAMAN!

THUNK

PARDON ME!

MY SHOP!

I'M VERY SORRY. HERE, TAKE THIS FOR THE DAMAGE.

HAVEN'T LOST MY TOUCH.

AHHH!

OW...

Eh?

STAY WHERE YOU ARE. I HAVE ONLY TO CRY OUT AND THOSE SOLDIERS WILL BE UPON YOU.

WHY SHOULD YOU WISH HARM ON A STRANGER WHO HAS CAUSED YOU NONE?

I SUPPOSE YOU ARE INNOCENT-- LIKE EVERY THIEF IN THE KING'S DUNGEONS.

WHAT DO YOU KNOW OF THE KING'S DUNGEONS?

BY GOD, YOU ARE LIKE THE FULL MOON RISING IN A CLEAR HEAVEN.

THIS WAY!

FORGIVE ME, BUT I CAN'T ALLOW THOSE GUARDS TO CATCH ME.

MY FEET HURT, AND I SIMPLY CAN'T RUN ANYMORE. I--

TOUCH ME AGAIN, AND YOUR ACHING FEET WILL BE THE LEAST OF YOUR WORRIES, I PROMISE.

PLEASE LIFT YOUR BLADE BEFORE IT SLIPS.

WHY WERE THOSE GUARDS CHASING YOU?

IT'S A LONG STORY.

AND YOU?

WHO ARE *YOU* RUNNING FROM?

WHO SAID I WAS RUNNING FROM ANYONE?

THAT CLOAK YOU'RE WEARING-- IT ISN'T YOURS. BUT THE CLOTHES UNDERNEATH DEFINITELY ARE.

YOU'RE SOMEBODY'S WIFE OR DAUGHTER. NO ONE WHO BOUGHT YOU THAT KIND OF JEWELRY WOULD LET YOU GO WITHOUT AN ESCORT IN THIS PART OF TOWN.

I'M NOT JUDGING. I'M JUST SAYING: I CAN ASK QUESTIONS TOO.

DAUGHTER.

WHAT?

I'M SOMEBODY'S DAUGHTER. AND I'M RUNNING AWAY FROM SOMEBODY. THERE. SATISFIED?

NO.

SO, PRINCESS! YOU THINK BECAUSE YOU'RE TOO BIG TO THRASH NOW, YOU CAN DO AS YOU PLEASE?

BAHRAM, I'M SORRY! I JUST WANTED TO SEE THE SWORD SWALLOWERS!

THE KING WOULD HAVE MY HEAD IF HE FOUND OUT ABOUT THIS!

LET'S GO!

"PRINCESS"?

"SHE HAD EYES LIKE DARK ALMONDS. LIPS LIKE POMEGRANATES. HER WAIST WOULD SHAME A BRONZE SPEAR, HER FIGURE THE WILLOW BOUGH.

"TRY AS I MIGHT, I COULDN'T GET HER OUT OF MY MIND."

"I GOT A JOB IN THE KING'S STABLES. I'VE ALWAYS BEEN GOOD WITH HORSES.

"I KNEW ONE DAY *SHE* WOULD WALK IN.

"WHEN SHE RODE, THE SADNESS SHE WORE LIKE A VEIL SEEMED TO LEAVE HER AND HER FACE GLOWED WITH JOY. SHE RODE LIKE THE WIND. I'D NEVER SEEN A WOMAN RIDE LIKE THAT.

"BY THE END OF THE MONTH WE WERE RIDING TOGETHER ALMOST EVERY DAY, IN THE HILLS ABOVE THE CITY. AND I WAS IN LOVE.

"BUT THE BOLDNESS THAT HAD SEIZED ME IN THE CITY WAS GONE. IT WAS AS IF THAT KISS HAD NEVER HAPPENED. AS THE DAYS AND WEEKS PASSED, I BEGAN TO FEEL I MUST HAVE DREAMT IT.

"SHE WAS SO COOL, UNTOUCHABLE-- SO ACHINGLY BEAUTIFUL. WITH EACH PASSING DAY HER MANNER TOWARD ME SEEMED TO GROW COLDER.

"I BECAME CONVINCED THAT SHE VIEWED ME WITH CONTEMPT. MY LOVE TORMENTED ME.

"THERE'S NOT MUCH MORE TO TELL."

"I LEARNED AT LAST THE REASON FOR HER SADNESS AND RESERVE. HER FATHER'S GRAND VIZIER, JAFFAR, WISHED TO MARRY HER.

"UNTIL NOW, THE KING, WHO LOVED HIS DAUGHTER TENDERLY, HAD HEEDED HER PLEAS AND HAD NOT SAID YES.

"BUT HE NEVER SAID NO. NOW THE KING AND HER BROTHERS WERE WITH THE ARMY IN KOSHKHAN.

"AS THE WAR DRAGGED ON AND THEY DID NOT RETURN, JAFFAR'S INFLUENCE GREW. HE BEGAN TO VISIT THE PRINCESS EVERY DAY WITH GIFTS AND DECLARATIONS OF HIS LOVE.

"JAFFAR'S IMPATIENCE WAS GROWING. SHE FEARED THAT HE WOULD SOON TAKE MATTERS INTO HIS OWN HANDS.

"WHEN SHE TOLD ME THIS MY FOREHEAD BURNED WITH ANGER. I WISHED FOR A SWORD, THAT I MIGHT KILL THIS VILLAIN.

"BUT WHAT COULD I DO? A STRANGER-- PENNILESS--WITH NO OTHER FRIEND IN SIRAF BUT THE ONE I WOULD GLADLY DIE FOR."

MY FATHER GAVE THIS BRACELET TO MY MOTHER WHEN THEY FIRST MET.

MAY ITS CHARMS PROTECT YOU WHO ARE DEARER TO ME THAN MYSELF.

"HOW COULD I KNOW IT WAS THE LAST TIME I WOULD SEE HER?

"WE RODE BACK TO THE STABLES SEPARATELY, AS WE ALWAYS DID. LIKE A FOOL, I WAS LOST IN DAYDREAMS."

"THEY THREW ME IN CHAINS THAT NIGHT.

"THAT WAS HOW I MET HIM.

"JAFFAR. THE GRAND VIZIER."

A THIEF WHO SNEAKS AND STEALS UNDER COVER OF NIGHT DOES NOT DESERVE DAYLIGHT.

DO WITH HIM WHAT YOU WILL... ONLY MAKE SURE THAT HE NEVER SEES THE SUN AGAIN.

I HEAR AND I OBEY, EXCELLENCY.

I TRUST, *BAHRAM*, THAT YOU WILL CARRY OUT THIS DUTY WITH GREATER DILIGENCE THAN YOU SHOWED IN PROTECTING THE PRINCESS.

"ONE LOOK AT HIM AND I KNEW THIS WAS THE MAN SHE HAD TOLD ME ABOUT.

"HE BARELY EVEN GLANCED AT ME. TO HIM I WAS OF NO MORE IMPORTANCE THAN A RAT CAUGHT IN THE KITCHEN AND TOSSED OUT WITH THE GARBAGE."

THEY BEAT ME UP AND THREW ME IN HERE. IT WOULD HAVE BEEN KINDER TO KILL ME. I CAN'T STOP THINKING ABOUT HER--WITH *HIM*--

AH WELL-- IT DOESN'T DO TO WEEP FOR LONG OVER A WOMAN, FOR THERE ARE AS MANY OF THEM AS THERE ARE STARS IN THE SKY. STILL, YOUR TALE IS DISTURBING.

I SHOULD HOPE SO.

THIS VIZIER ORDERED YOU PUT WHERE YOU WOULDN'T SEE DAYLIGHT AGAIN.

BUT *I* AM HERE ONLY TEMPORARILY, TO AWAIT MY APPOINTMENT WITH THE GOVERNOR. IT DOESN'T MAKE SENSE THAT THEY PUT US IN THE SAME CELL.

BREAKFAST ALREADY!

TALKING DOES MAKE THE TIME PASS FASTER.

WHY DIDN'T YOU TELL ME SOONER? I COULD HAVE SAVED HOURS!

CAREFUL... DON'T BREAK THE BLADE.

WITH THE AID OF A DAGGER, WHICH I HAD UNWITTINGLY FORGOTTEN TO TURN OVER TO THE GUARDS WHEN THEY RELIEVED ME OF MY OTHER POSSESSIONS, THE YOUTH AND I SUCCEEDED IN LOOSENING A STONE THE SIZE OF A MAN'S HEAD.

THIS IS A VERY BAD IDEA.

WHEN THE GUARDS SEE WHAT YOU'VE DONE THEY'LL PUNISH US BOTH. IT WILL COUNT AGAINST ME WITH THE GOVERNOR.

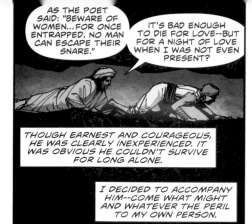

AS THE POET SAID: "BEWARE OF WOMEN...FOR ONCE ENTRAPPED, NO MAN CAN ESCAPE THEIR SNARE."

IT'S BAD ENOUGH TO DIE FOR LOVE--BUT FOR A NIGHT OF LOVE WHEN I WAS NOT EVEN PRESENT?

I THINK WE MAY HAVE A PROBLEM...

THOUGH EARNEST AND COURAGEOUS, HE WAS CLEARLY INEXPERIENCED. IT WAS OBVIOUS HE COULDN'T SURVIVE FOR LONG ALONE.

I DECIDED TO ACCOMPANY HIM--COME WHAT MIGHT AND WHATEVER THE PERIL TO MY OWN PERSON.

AAHH!!

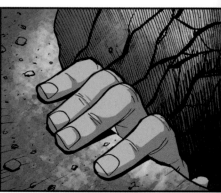

COME ON...

UP YOU GO!

YOU'RE NOT VERY GOOD WITH A SWORD, ARE YOU?

I'M NEW AT IT. I'LL GET BETTER WITH PRACTICE.

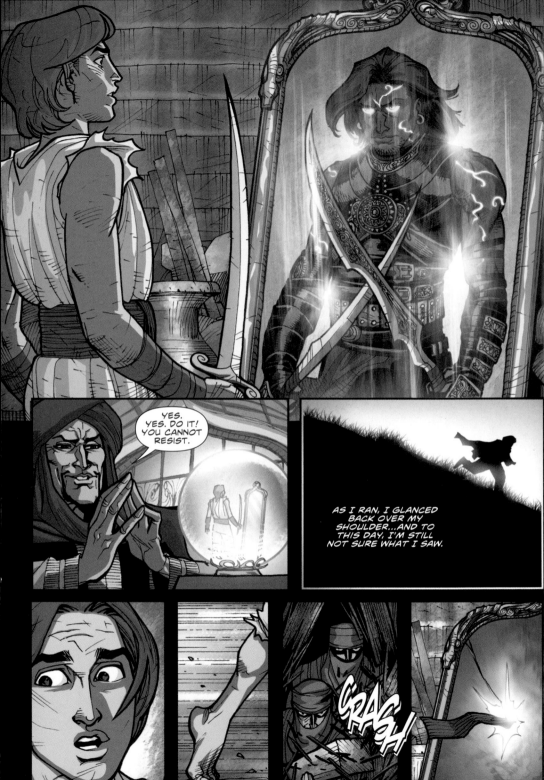

MY NAME IS SESO.

SESO'S TALE
Art by David Lopez

I WAS BORN FAR FROM HERE, IN AFRICA. I LOST MY FATHER YOUNG. MY UNCLES TAUGHT ME TO HUNT.

THE DAY MY LIFE ENDED BEGAN LIKE ANY OTHER DAY.

THERE HAD BEEN NO SIGN. THE ANCESTORS DID NOT FOREWARN US.

TO BE SEPARATED FOREVER FROM THOSE WE LOVE TAKES ONLY A MOMENT.

LIKE A KNIFE BLADE, DIVIDING THE LIFE WE KNEW FROM THE ONE THAT IS TO COME.

THIS IS HOW
IT HAPPENS.
IN A MOMENT.
WITHOUT
WARNING.

I KNOW NOW THAT THIS IS THE WAY OF THE WORLD.

MANY DIED CROSSING THE DESERT. I WISHED TO DIE, BUT I DID NOT.

I WAS BOUGHT BY AN EGYPTIAN TRADER. HIS SHIP WAS CROWDED WITH CAMELS AND CAPTIVES OF DIFFERENT TRIBES.

WE SAILED SOUTH TO ADEN. THERE I WAS SOLD AGAIN.

AFTER MANY DAYS AND NIGHTS AT SEA, WE MADE PORT IN A CITY CALLED SUR.

THAT WAS THE DAY MY LIFE BEGAN AGAIN. THE DAY I MET THE MAN WHO STANDS BEFORE YOU--*SHEIKH AMAR.*

YOU. GET OUT.

THIS IS AN OUTRAGE! MY MONEY IS AS GOOD AS ANYONE'S!

OF ALL THE MERCHANTS IN THE MARKETPLACE THAT DAY, THIS MAN DREW MY ATTENTION FROM THE FIRST MOMENT.

THE COINS YOU GAVE ME LAST TIME WERE AS FALSE AS THAT STORY YOU GAVE MY COUSIN.

GET HIM OUT OF HERE.

AH!

HIS CHARACTER WAS EVIDENT TO ALL IN THE RESPECT WITH WHICH OTHERS TREATED HIM.

HONESTY AND NOBILITY WERE WRITTEN ON HIS FACE.

THAT ONE! I'LL PAY FIFTY DIRHAMS FOR HIM!

NO...

I DARED TO HOPE THAT THIS GOOD, NOBLE MAN MIGHT PURCHASE ME AND BECOME MY MASTER.

WHAT AM I BID FOR THIS FINE FIGURE OF A MAN? A *NGBAKA* FROM THE HEART OF SUDAN. STRONG. HEALTHY.

FORTY DIRHAMS.

FORTY-FIVE.

FIFTY DIRHAMS!

SHUT UP, YOU.

FIFTY DIRHAMS.

SIXTY!

SIXTY DIRHAMS! TRUE PERSIAN DIRHAMS FROM NASAF!

MAY MY OWN MOTHER DISOWN ME IF I'M LYING!

THE BID IS FIFTY DIRHAMS.

DO I HEAR FIFTY-FIVE? GOING... GOING...

SOLD FOR FIFTY DIRHAMS!

YOU WANT TO KNOW WHAT'S WRONG WITH PERSIA TODAY? FAVORITISM! THE PRIVILEGED FEW LINING THEIR POCKETS WITH SWEETHEART TRANSACTIONS. A MAN OF ENTERPRISE DOESN'T STAND A CHANCE.

SO GENEROUS WAS HE, THAT HE REMOVED HIMSELF FROM THE BIDDING WHEN HE SAW ANOTHER WANTED ME.

IN THIS WAY I ENTERED THE SERVICE OF THE MERCHANT FARUQ.

AS FOR SHEIKH AMAR...DESTINY HAD DECREED THAT OUR PATHS WERE TO CROSS AGAIN.

MONTHS PASSED. THE LANGUAGE OF THE PERSIANS, STRANGE AT FIRST, BEGAN TO SOUND FAMILIAR TO MY EARS.

I BECAME ACCUSTOMED TO MY NEW LIFE. A CONDITION THAT I HAD ONCE SEEN AS WORSE THAN DEATH NOW SEEMED NORMAL.

THIS, TOO, IS THE WAY OF THE WORLD.

ONE DAY A GREAT EXCITEMENT SEIZED THE HOUSEHOLD LIKE A FEVER. MY MASTER'S COUSIN, A VIZIER IN THE COURT OF A PERSIAN KING, WAS COMING TO VISIT.

HE WAS BRINGING ONE OF HIS DAUGHTERS TO BE MARRIED TO MY MASTER'S SON. A GREAT HONOR AND BLESSING FOR THE FAMILY.

WEEKS WERE SPENT GETTING READY FOR THE BANQUET. MY MASTER WAS DETERMINED THAT EVERYTHING SHOULD BE OF THE BEST QUALITY, FROM THE PORCELAIN DISHES TO THE ROSE PETALS IN THE FOUNTAINS...

...TO THE GARMENTS WORN BY HIS SERVANTS.

NATURALLY, THE ENTERTAINMENT ALSO HAD TO BE OF THE BEST. THE CITY OF SUR BEING WELL KNOWN FOR ITS MUSICIANS AND PERFORMERS...

LOOK, A WEDDING! WHAT AN OPPORTUNITY!

I DON'T KNOW, SHEIKH...REMEMBER WHAT HAPPENED LAST TIME WITH THE DANCING GIRLS AND THE ELEPHANTS?

BAH! THAT WAS A FUNERAL--ENTIRELY DIFFERENT, BEMBE.

THIS IS A HAPPY OCCASION. THE GUESTS WILL BE GRATEFUL FOR A LITTLE DIVERSION. TRUST ME, EVERYONE LOVES A CIRCUS.

AT WEDDING PARTIES PEOPLE SCATTER GOLD LIKE RICE. ALL WE NEED TO DO IS BE THERE TO CATCH IT.

...WHO WOULD HE TURN TO, WHO WOULD HE TRUST, BUT SHEIKH AMAR-- THAT MOST REPUTABLE OF MEN?

A BANQUET LIKE THAT, THE GUARDS WON'T LET US NEAR!

WE'LL SEND KAILEENA IN FIRST. SHE'S A GREAT NEGOTIATOR. BEMBE, YOU WORRY TOO MUCH.

NOT AGAIN...

LOOK AT THAT OSTRICH! WHAT A BEAUTY!

AS FOR ME, I HAD A PROBLEM...

WHEN MY MASTER'S HONORED GUESTS ARRIVED FOR THE WEDDING--KAZI, I AM ASHAMED TO SAY THIS; BUT A MAN'S LIFE IS AT STAKE, AND I HAVE SWORN TO TELL THE WHOLE TRUTH--

MY FRIEND!

ALLOW ME TO PRESENT...

...MY WIFE AND DAUGHTER.

FOR SOME STRANGE REASON, THE LADY WIFE OF THIS GREAT VIZIER...

...CONCEIVED A LIKING FOR ME, A SLAVE.

FROM THE FIRST MOMENT, I KNEW I WAS IN DANGER.

NOT LEAST OF THE ATTRACTIONS WAS THE RARE CHANCE TO SEE THE FAMED TRAVELING CIRCUS OF SHEIKH AMAR. EVERYONE WAS TALKING ABOUT IT.

HOW COULD YOU LET THAT STREET FILTH IN HERE?!?

I THOUGHT THEY WERE PART OF THE PROGRAM. COME ON, THEY'RE NOT SO BAD.

THANKS! SEE YOU LATER...

ARE YOU HAVING A GOOD TIME?

GOOD, GOOD, CARRY ON! DON'T MISS THE KNIFE THROWER-- HE'LL BE ON SOON. I HEAR HE'S INCREDIBLE!

WHO IS HE?

I RECOGNIZED SHEIKH AMAR AMONG THE GUESTS. I NOTICED THAT AS HE MOVED THROUGH THIS ELITE GATHERING, THERE WAS HARDLY A MAN OR WOMAN PRESENT WHO DID NOT TAKE NOTE OF HIM.

AH! HERE HE IS NOW! BEMBE THE NGBAKA, MASTER OF THE THROWING KNIFE!

WIELDING BLADES SAID TO BE BLESSED BY THE CREATOR HIMSELF! WHAT A PRIVILEGE TO SEE THIS, WHAT A TREAT!

SOMEONE IN THAT TENT OVER THERE ASKED FOR ROSE WATER.

HURRY UP, I'VE GOT MY HANDS FULL.

IT WAS THEN THAT DISASTER STRUCK.

45

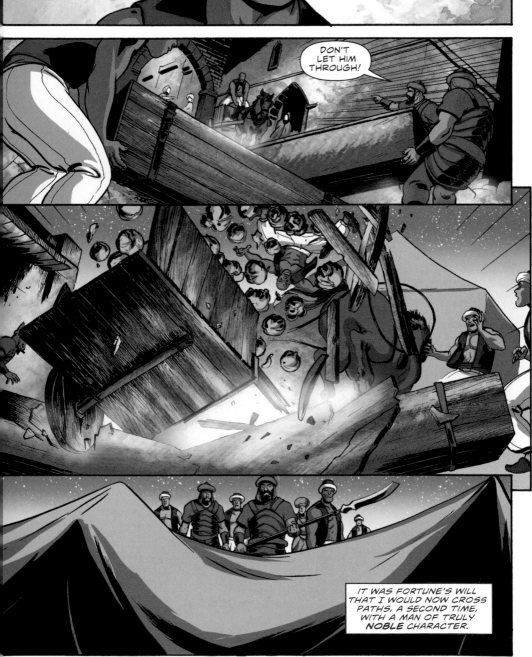

HE CAN'T BE FAR! FIND HIM!

A GENEROUS MAN WHO ABHORS INJUSTICE AND SEEKS ONLY TO HELP OTHERS...

PLEASE LET ME HIDE HERE.

GET OUT! OUT OF HERE! NOW!

...THIS MAN... SHEIKH AMAR.

IF YOU HIDE ME I'LL PAY YOU. I CAN WORK.

IT'S YOU! NGBAKA!

NGBAKA, CAN YOU THROW KNIVES?

KNIVES? YES.

PUT ON THESE CLOTHES. YOU'RE HIRED.

BE QUICK, NGBAKA. I'D BE GLAD TO LINGER, BUT MY CIRCUMSTANCES ON THIS PARTICULAR EVENING ARE LESS THAN IDEAL, IF YOU GET MY DRIFT.

IN MY DESPERATE SITUATION, NO ORDINARY MAN COULD SAVE ME. ONLY A PERSON OF IMPECCABLE HONESTY AND PIETY COULD SPEAK FOR ME AND BE BELIEVED.

YOU! SLAVE!

I BEG YOUR PARDON. WHY ARE YOU MANHANDLING MY ASSOCIATE?

MY KNIFE THROWER.

ASSOCIATE?

HE LOOKS LIKE THE SLAVE WHO ESCAPED.

HE CAN HARDLY BE THE MAN YOU'RE LOOKING FOR, WHEN HE'S JUST FINISHED PERFORMING IN FULL VIEW OF THE COMPANY.

NGBAKA, DEMONSTRATE YOUR TALENTS.

SEE THAT FIG TREE? WATCH, HE'S GOING TO HIT IT.

GO! SEE IF HE HIT IT!

FWT

NORMALLY, I'D BE GLAD TO LINGER...

...BUT YOU GENTLEMEN HAVE A FUGITIVE SLAVE TO PURSUE...AND WE HAVE BUSINESS TO ATTEND TO. GOOD LUCK.

SUCH WAS THE RESPECT THIS MAN COMMANDED, THAT UPON HEARING HIM SAY HE BELIEVED I WAS INNOCENT, EVERYONE PRESENT IMMEDIATELY ACCEPTED HIS WORD.

DON'T LOOK BACK, *NGBAKA*. WE'RE NOT IN THE CLEAR YET.

WHEN I WAS A LITTLE GIRL, I SPENT SOME TIME WITH MY MOTHER'S AUNT IN THE HAREM OF THE **GRAND VIZIER BARTOL.**

I LOVED THE FUSS THE WOMEN MADE OVER ME. THEY'D SIT FOR HOURS BRUSHING MY HAIR, LIKE A LITTLE DOLL. SO DIFFERENT FROM BACK HOME.

BUT WHAT I LOVED BEST WAS THE EVENINGS WHEN THE WOMEN WOULD SIT UP LATE TELLING STORIES.

IT WAS ON MY LAST NIGHT, BEFORE I LEFT, THAT AN OLD WOMAN NAMED **FARAH** CONSENTED TO TELL HER STORY. THE ONE I'D BEEN BEGGING FOR BUT SHE'D ALWAYS REFUSED.

MY PARENTS SOLD ME WHEN I WAS FIFTEEN YEARS OLD.

A BEDOUIN TOOK ME AWAY.

IT WAS A HARD JOURNEY. I WAS LONELY AND FRIGHTENED, BUT I CAN'T SAY I WAS EVER MISTREATED.

WHEN THE SUN WAS STRONG THEY GAVE ME SHADE. WHEN WE RAN SHORT OF FOOD AND WATER, THEY WENT WITHOUT SO THAT I MIGHT EAT.

DINARZAD'S TALE
Art by Niko Henrichon

BUT THEY WITHHELD WHAT I WAS MOST STARVED FOR. A KIND WORD, A FRIENDLY LOOK. THEY TREATED ME LIKE AN OBJECT-- A RARE BIRD OR A VALUABLE HORSE.

NO, LESS THAN THAT. BECAUSE YOU TALK TO A HORSE. YOU GIVE IT A PAT ON THE NECK. THEY NEVER TOUCHED ME.

THEY WOULDN'T EVEN LOOK AT ME.

SOMETIMES, I WAS SURE I FELT THE EYES OF HIS SLAVE ON ME. HE WAS A BOY NOT MUCH OLDER THAN I.

BUT PERHAPS THAT WAS WISHFUL THINKING.

IN THE BEGINNING I WEPT OFTEN. THEN I STOPPED WEEPING. IT WAS A WASTE OF WATER.

WE ARRIVED AT A FORTRESS. BY THIS TIME, I FELT NOTHING. NOT FEAR, NOT HOPE.

THEY PAID THE BEDOUIN. THREE GOLD COINS AND HE LEFT WITHOUT A WORD. THAT WAS THE LAST I SAW OF HIM.

NEVER IN A THOUSAND YEARS COULD I HAVE IMAGINED WHAT LAY BEHIND THAT DOOR.

LOOK, HE'S AWAKE!

HE'S SO HANDSOME!

HE IS MORE THAN A HERO, HE IS A GOD IN MY EYES...

THE MAN WHO IS ALLOWED TO SIT BESIDE YOU...

HE WHO LISTENS INTIMATELY TO THE SWEET MURMUR OF YOUR VOICE...

THE ENTICING LAUGHTER THAT MAKES MY OWN HEART BEAT FAST...

IT WAS FUN FOR US, HAVING A SPECIAL NIGHT ONCE IN A WHILE.

WHAT IT MUST HAVE BEEN LIKE FOR THE BOYS, I CAN ONLY IMAGINE.

SOONER OR LATER THEY FELL ASLEEP, LULLED BY THE WINE AND THE KASH.

THAT'S WHEN THE EUNUCHS WOULD COME AND TAKE THEM AWAY. ONE NIGHT IN PARADISE. THAT'S ALL THEY GOT.

ME? MY PARADISE LASTED SIX MONTHS.

IF I HAD IT ALL TO DO OVER AGAIN, WOULD I MAKE THE SAME CHOICE? I HONESTLY DON'T KNOW.

THE OLDER I GET, THE LONGER I LIVE, THE MORE I REALIZE HOW RARE IT IS IN LIFE TO FIND EVEN A LITTLE BIT OF PARADISE.

WHEN YOU'RE YOUNG, YOU DON'T THINK ABOUT SUCH THINGS. YOU SEE SOMETHING YOU WANT, YOU REACH OUT AND TAKE IT.

FARAH!

IT'S ME-- NABU.

I RAN AWAY FROM THE BEDOUIN. IT TOOK ME THREE MONTHS TO GET BACK HERE AND THREE MORE TO FIGURE OUT A WAY IN.

I SWORE TO MYSELF I WOULDN'T ABANDON YOU HERE. THAT I'D COME BACK AND RESCUE YOU.

RESCUE ME? NABU...

I LOVE YOU, FARAH. I'VE LOVED YOU FROM THE FIRST MOMENT I SAW YOU.

ME TOO. I THINK. FROM THE FIRST MOMENT.

NABU HAD WORKED OUT OUR ESCAPE PLAN. THE NEXT FEW HOURS WERE LIKE AN ETERNITY FOR ME... HAVING TO BEHAVE NORMALLY WITH THE OTHER GIRLS, WAITING FOR NIGHT TO FALL.

I MET HIM AT THE PLACE HE'D SHOWN ME, BY THE SIDE WALL. SEEING HIM THERE WAITING, WITH A ROPE--IT WAS THE HAPPIEST MOMENT OF MY LIFE.

MY HEART WAS BEATING SO HARD, I WAS SURE THE GUARDS COULD HEAR IT.

ALMOST THERE. ONCE WE'RE PAST THAT TOWER, WE'RE HOME FREE.

BOOM BOOM BOOM

FARAH, COME ON!

BOOM BOOM

WHAT I SAW THEN CHILLED MY BLOOD, AS I REALIZED THE TERRIBLE PURPOSE FOR WHICH THE OTHER GIRLS AND I WERE BEING USED.

THESE WERE NO ORDINARY SOLDIERS.

I'LL FIND WORK IN SAMARKAND. MY PEOPLE THERE WILL HELP US. I'LL PROTECT YOU.

I'VE OFTEN WONDERED ABOUT THE STRANGE ALCHEMY THAT TRANSFORMS A MAN SO THAT HE IS WILLING TO DIE FOR SOMETHING.

NABU, HURRY!

HOW DOES AN IDEA, A DREAM--OR ANOTHER PERSON-- BECOME MORE IMPORTANT THAN OUR OWN LIFE?

NABU!

I SUPPOSE YOU'RE GOING TO TELL ME OF SOME NOBLE ACTION YOUR SISTER DID WHEN SHE WAS IN THE CRADLE.

NO, EXCELLENCY. I ONLY WANT TO SUGGEST A POSSIBILITY THAT NONE OF US HAS CONSIDERED.

HAS IT NOT JUST BEEN ANNOUNCED THAT PRINCE DASTAN IS TO MARRY?

WOULD IT NOT MAKE SENSE FOR THE PRINCE TO HONOR HIS NEW BRIDE BY REWARDING SOMEONE *SHE* FAVORS? SOMEONE WHO PERFORMED A SERVICE FOR *HER* LONG AGO?

CONTINUE.

SHARZAD'S TALE
Art by Tommy Lee Edwards

Since I was a child, I have heard tales of the sacred city of Alamut, a place favored by the gods.

Though the valley in which it lies is lush and green, no army has ever breached its walls. Even the Turanian hordes passed it by out of respect.

It is said that Alamut is the place where time began.

One would have to live in a remote village indeed not to have heard of Princess TAMINA of Alamut.

I know from my friend PADMA, who married my cousin's brother, that tales of the Princess's beauty and goodness are not exaggerated.

Padma was Princess Tamina's childhood companion. She told me that even then, her face was like the sun and the moon, and radiated such purity that it would make a holy man lower his eyes. In short, it is no wonder that our Prince DASTAN chose her as his bride.

She told me a good deal more besides.

Alamut was their playground--a garden of delights.

As the Princess's best friend, Padma was showered with favors. Her parents were well taken care of.

Hearing her tales, how I wished my childhood had been even just a little bit like hers!

But all good things must end.

On Tamina's ninth birthday, the Regent of Alamut sent her to the Hidden Valley to be educated by the GUARDIANS.

Why they're called that, I don't know. Padma said that when she asked what they were guarding, the adults got vague and changed the subject.

I do know that the journey was long and arduous. That when the two best friends said good-bye, both understood it was for the last time.

YOU MAY GO.

YOU ARE VERY LIKE YOUR MOTHER.

There is a legend of ALAMUT...

Long ago, in the time before time, the sun god looked down and saw the selfish wickedness of man. It made him angry. The light became darkness in his sight. And so he sent a great sandstorm to destroy all--blot out the sun and wipe clean the face of the earth.

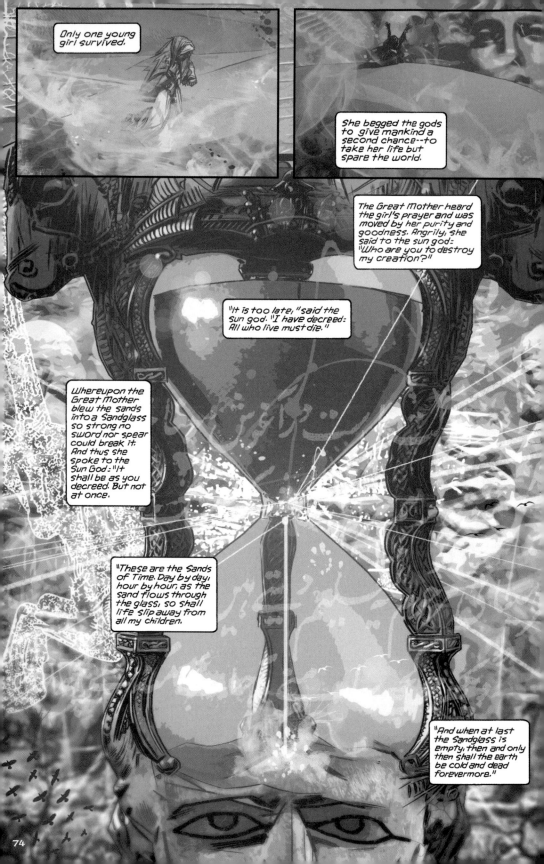

Only one young girl survived.

She begged the gods to give mankind a second chance--to take her life but spare the world.

The Great Mother heard the girl's prayer and was moved by her purity and goodness. Angrily, she said to the sun god: "Who are you to destroy my creation?"

"It is too late," said the sun god. "I have decreed: All who live must die."

Whereupon the Great Mother blew the sands into a Sandglass so strong no sword nor spear could break it. And thus she spoke to the Sun God: "It shall be as you decreed. But not at once.

"These are the Sands of Time. Day by day, hour by hour, as the sand flows through the glass, so shall life slip away from all my children.

"And when at last the Sandglass is empty, then and only then shall the earth be cold and dead forevermore."

That girl who won mankind its reprieve lived a long time and had many children.

The *GUARDIANS* are her descendants. They are the royal family of Alamut--the priests of its temple. This was Tamina's destiny. Her calling, passed down by blood.

This, and more, she learned in her first weeks in the Hidden Valley.

I DON'T WANT TO PEEL TURNIPS. I WANT TO GO HOME.

MY CHILD, THIS *IS* YOUR HOME.

IT IS *NOT!* MY HOME IS ALAMUT! I'M GOING BACK THERE--AND DON'T TRY TO STOP ME!

WHAT WILL I TELL THE KING ???

So angry was Tamina--so good did it feel to have the wind in her hair, the thrill of freedom--that she was a half-day's ride from the Hidden Valley before it occurred to her to be afraid.

It was a week's journey to Alamut. And she was a girl--unarmed, alone. Riding a thoroughbred mare that many men might consider more valuable than a human life.

As she rode, she wondered: Were those her own horse's hoof steps she heard echoing off the rock walls--or another rider's?

When she stopped, the sound stopped.

When she started, it started again.

It was no echo.

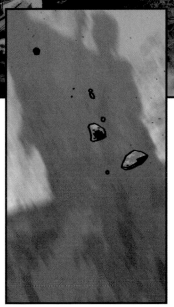

WHO'S THERE?

I WARN YOU--I'M A WARRIOR! I'LL CUT YOU INTO LITTLE PIECES!

She reasoned that there was, at least, some additional safety in numbers --however small.

His name was ASOKA, a slave who had run away from his harsh master after one beating too many.

WHERE DID YOU GET THAT PONY?

HE'S NOT A PONY. HE'S A MOUNTAIN HORSE.

I STOLE HIM IN THE MARKET. HE'S A LOT FASTER THAN YOUR STUPID HORSE.

IN OTHER WORDS, YOU'RE NOT ONLY RUDE, YOU'RE A THIEF.

YOU'D BETTER WATCH YOUR TONGUE. I DEFEATED THREE WARRIORS TO GET THIS HORSE.

ACTUALLY, SIX, THEY HAD SWORDS. AND KNIVES.

WHAT DID YOU FIGHT THEM WITH? THAT STICK?

I'M GOOD AT SWORD FIGHTING. THE BEST.

I'M SURE YOU ARE.

She soon came to regret her decision.

Though she gave him every chance, he stubbornly refused to rejoin her. Yet neither did he lose sight of her.

The days wore on. They rode without encountering another soul.

Tamina found herself missing Asoka's company--annoying as it had been.

Then there came a moment when she looked back and he wasn't there.

She waited. Still, he did not come.

PRINCESS TAMINA?

YOU-- RIDE BACK TO ALAMUT, TELL THE KING WE'VE FOUND HER.

The king's anger at his daughter's rebellion was over-whelmed by relief at having her home safe.

Padma, of course, was overjoyed.

ASOKA! STOP SPYING ON US!

I'M NOT SPYING. I WAS HERE FIRST. TALK SOMEWHERE ELSE.

But not for long.

I'M GOING TO BE THE GREATEST WARRIOR OF ALAMUT. THEY'RE ALREADY TEACHING ME.

ASOKA, WOULD YOU LEAVE ME IN PEACE FOR JUST FIVE MINUTES?

It was Tamina who asked her father to send her back to the Hidden Valley to continue her Priestess training--to every-one's surprise.

A king of old once counseled: "Do not act as if you were going to live ten thousand years. Death stands at your elbow. Be good for some-thing, while you live and it is in your power."

Was it Tamina's brush with death that had matured her? Had she felt, at that tender age, the chill breath of the Sands of Time flowing through their glass--and realized that her days, too, were finite as the grains in a handful of sand?

Or was it some quality in the slave boy Asoka that had made her see her own life and obligations in a different light?

I only know what Padma told me. She never saw her friend again. They had different destinies.

As do we all, Your Excellency.

MY VILLAGE OF **BASH**, IN THE MOUNTAINS NORTH OF NASAF, IS FAMOUS FOR MANY REASONS...

BUT PERHAPS THE MAIN REASON IS MY BROTHER'S WIFE'S COUSIN **ROHAM**.

I WAS ONLY A BOY WHEN ROHAM LEFT TO FIGHT IN THE ARMY OF OUR GREAT **KING SHARAMAN,** MAY HE LIVE TEN THOUSAND YEARS.

THE PORTER'S TALE
Art by Cameron Stewart

THREE YEARS HAD PASSED WITH NO NEWS. YOU CAN IMAGINE THE EXCITEMENT ON THE DAY ROHAM CAME HOME TO VISIT.

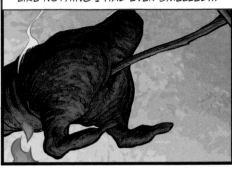

I WAS MORE INTERESTED IN THE SUCCULENT *LAMB*, WHICH ROHAM HAD SEASONED WITH A SUBTLE MIX OF SPICES LIKE NOTHING I HAD EVER SMELLED...

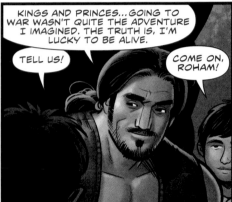

HAVE YOU MET THE KING?

WHAT ABOUT THE PRINCES?

WHAT'S HE LIKE?

WHICH ONE IS THE BETTER FIGHTER--*TUS* OR *GARSIV*?

OR *DASTAN*?

KINGS AND PRINCES...GOING TO WAR WASN'T QUITE THE ADVENTURE I IMAGINED. THE TRUTH IS, I'M LUCKY TO BE ALIVE.

TELL US!

COME ON, ROHAM!

THAT NIGHT, AFTER A MEAL I REMEMBER AS IF I HAD TASTED IT ONLY YESTERDAY, ROHAM GAVE IN TO OUR ENTREATIES.

OUR GOOD KING *SHARAMAN*, THE LION OF PERSIA, MAY HE LIVE TEN THOUSAND YEARS, SENT A FLEET TO AID THE KING OF YEMEN, WHOSE CITY WAS UNDER SIEGE BY ARABS...

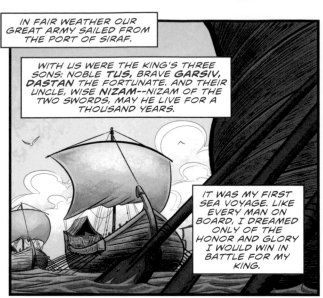

IN FAIR WEATHER OUR GREAT ARMY SAILED FROM THE PORT OF SIRAF.

WITH US WERE THE KING'S THREE SONS: NOBLE **TUS**, BRAVE **GARSIV**, **DASTAN** THE FORTUNATE. AND THEIR UNCLE, WISE **NIZAM**--NIZAM OF THE TWO SWORDS, MAY HE LIVE FOR A THOUSAND YEARS.

IT WAS MY FIRST SEA VOYAGE. LIKE EVERY MAN ON BOARD, I DREAMED ONLY OF THE HONOR AND GLORY I WOULD WIN IN BATTLE FOR MY KING.

SUCH VAIN THOUGHTS SOON VANISHED AS THE SEAS TURNED ROUGH.

LATER, WE LEARNED THAT IT WAS THE DEMON **AHRIMAN** WHO HAD SENT THE STORM AT THE BIDDING OF AN ARABIAN SORCERER...

BUT AT THE TIME, ALL WE KNEW WAS THAT OUR LIVES SUDDENLY HUNG BY THE THINNEST OF THREADS.

KRAK

WHEN I SAW THE STORM SMASH OUR MAST IN TWO, I GAVE MYSELF UP FOR DEAD.

I HAD SEEN OUR SHIP SINK BENEATH THE WAVES. I FELL TO MY KNEES AND THANKED GOD FOR SPARING MY LIFE.

HAD I KNOWN ON WHAT SHORE I HAD LANDED, I MIGHT WELL HAVE WISHED THAT I TOO HAD DROWNED WITH MY COMRADES.

OLD MAN! I'M STRONG. GIVE ME A MEAL AND I'LL PAY YOU TWICE ITS WORTH IN WORK.

GO AWAY.

IF YOU FEAR KING SHARAMAN, YOU SHOULD BE MORE POLITE TO A MAN IN HIS SERVICE.

OUR KING IS ZAHAK.

A STRONG MAN LIKE YOU HAD BETTER GET AS FAR AWAY FROM HERE AS HE CAN.

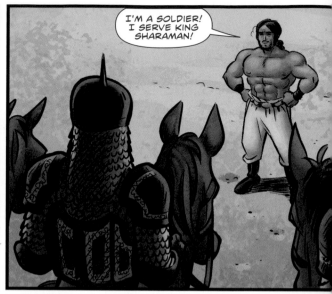

I'M A SOLDIER! I SERVE KING SHARAMAN!

THWIP

PAF

AND NOW YOU'LL SERVE KING ZAHAK. CONSIDER IT AN HONOR.

IT WAS THEN THAT I REALIZED. I'D SEEN ONLY OLD MEN, WOMEN, AND CHILDREN. IN ALL THE VILLAGE THERE WAS NOT ONE MAN IN THE PRIME OF LIFE.

HOW LONG WE RODE, I COULDN'T HAVE SAID. I WAS DELIRIOUS WITH HUNGER AND THIRST.

MY FIRST THOUGHT WHEN I WOKE WAS THAT I WAS STILL ON BOARD THE SHIP AND IT HAD ALL BEEN A NIGHTMARE.

BUT IT WAS A HORSE'S GAIT I FELT PITCHING ME FROM SIDE TO SIDE, NOT THE ROCKING OF THE WAVES.

KSSSH

FARHAD...?

ROHAM!

YOU SURVIVED THE WRECK?

SEVEN OF *US* CLUNG TO A PLANK AND FLOATED WITHIN SIGHT OF SHORE. A GALLEY PICKED US UP.

IF I'D KNOWN, I'D HAVE LET GO THE PLANK AND SUNK TO THE BOTTOM OF THE SEA.

IF YOU HAD KNOWN? KNOWN *WHAT?*

THAT ONE THERE. AND THAT ONE.

NOT ME! PLEASE... I BEG YOU...!

ARASH...
IF THERE WERE
SEVEN OF YOU, WHAT
HAPPENED TO THE
OTHERS?

EVERY
NIGHT HE
TAKES
TWO.

ZAHAK
TAKES
THEM.

AAAAARRRGGHHH NO NO NO

EEAAAAA

THE FIRST SCREAM
PULLED ME FROM SLEEP.
IT WENT ON AND ON.

AND THEN--
SILENCE.

THEY SAY ZAHAK MUST
BE FED EVERY NIGHT WITH
THE BRAINS OF TWO
STRONG MEN.

HIS GUARDS KNOW
THAT IF THEY FAIL
TO PROVIDE, IT'LL
BE THEIR TURN
NEXT.

WHAT KIND
OF KING IS
THIS?

AND YOU--
FOR TWO NIGHTS
YOU'VE SAT HERE
LIKE SHEEP, WHILE
OUR COMRADES GET
SLAUGHTERED?

WHAT
WOULD YOU
DO?

THE GUARDS FED US WELL, TO MAKE SURE WE WOULD BE FIT FOR ZAHAK.

THAT WAS THEIR FIRST MISTAKE.

BY NIGHTFALL OF THE SECOND DAY, I COULD FEEL MY STRENGTH RETURNING.

BEFORE THE GUARDS CAME, I HAD ARASH BIND MY WRISTS WITH A PIECE OF ROPE, DELIBERATELY FRAYED.

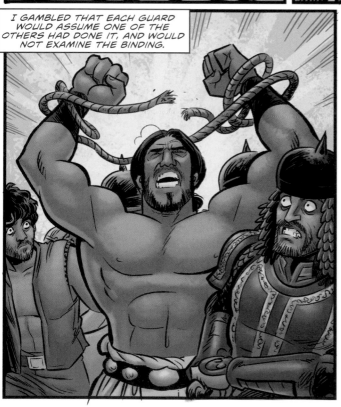

I GAMBLED THAT EACH GUARD WOULD ASSUME ONE OF THE OTHERS HAD DONE IT, AND WOULD NOT EXAMINE THE BINDING.

BAP

THAT WAS THEIR SECOND MISTAKE.

SLASH

SKLTCH

ARASH!!!

ROHAM...

SAVE YOURSELF. RUN.

AND THAT'S WHAT I DID. I RAN. I LEFT BRAVE ARASH AND MY OTHER SHIPMATES TO THEIR FATE.

I TOLD YOU THIS WASN'T A PRETTY TALE.

BY MIDDAY, I WAS EXHAUSTED AND HUNGRY.

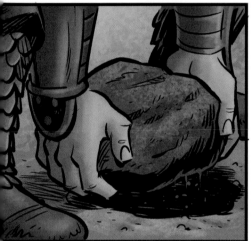

BY THE TIME I'D DESCENDED THE RAVINE TO WHERE THE BIRD HAD FALLEN, I WAS SWELTERING IN THE GUARD'S ARMOR AND CURSING MY LUCK.

SO GREAT WAS MY HUNGER, I COULD ALREADY SMELL THE BIRD ROASTING... ITS SKIN CRISPING... FRAGRANT JUICES FLOWING...

IT WASN'T MY IMAGINATION.

THAT BIRD IS MINE!

SO YOU'RE THE REASON IT FELL OUT OF THE SKY. NICE SHOT.

CARE TO JOIN US?

I HAVE A BETTER IDEA.

IF YOU TAKE OFF NOW, I'LL FORGET YOU STOLE MY FOOD.

LET'S BE REASONABLE...

THAT BIRD'S NOT VERY BIG TO BEGIN WITH.

IF WE WASTE OUR ENERGY FIGHTING, WE'LL END UP HUNGRIE THAN WE STARTED.

THAT IS WHY YOU SHOULD BE RUNNING.

YOU'VE GOT A SWORD AND WE DON'T. THAT HARDLY SEEMS FAIR.

BIS, HERE, WILL REFEREE. IF YOU CAN BEST ME ONE-ON-ONE, YOU CAN HAVE THE BIRD--NO HARD FEELINGS.

CHAK

I'VE TRAVELED A FAIR BIT...

...AND I HAVE TO SAY, THE PEOPLE ON THIS ISLAND...

KONK

...ARE SOME OF THE LEAST HOSPITABLE I'VE EVER ENCOUNTERED.

WHAM

YOU GOT THAT RIGHT.

DASTAN, LOOK OUT!

BIS, A REFEREE DOESN'T TAKE SIDES. THAT'S CALLED CHEATING.

I'M SORRY, YOUR HIGHNESS.

YOU'RE... PRINCE DASTAN?

YOU CAN GET UP NOW.

YOU WERE ON OUR SHIP?

I'M ROHAM, FROM BASH. YOUR HIGHNESS, HOW CAN I EVER EARN YOUR FORGIVENESS?

WELL, FOR ONE THING, YOU COULD PUT THAT MIGHTY ARM OF YOURS TO USE CATCHING US ANOTHER BIRD.

...STAN WASN'T ANYTHING LIKE D IMAGINED A PRINCE WOULD BE. VERY DOWN-TO-EARTH.

WE SPENT MOST OF THE EVENING TALKING ABOUT FOOD.

IF ONLY WE HAD SOME FRESH PEACHES, THAT WOULD MAKE THE MEAL COMPLETE.

I ATE A PEACH ONCE AS A BOY. SUCCULENT, JUICY...I REMEMBER IT AS IF I WERE BITING INTO IT RIGHT NOW. IT WAS THE MOST DELICIOUS THING I'VE EVER TASTED.

FOR ME, IT'S THE APRICOT CHICKEN MY GRANDFATHER USED TO MAKE.

AND YOU, MY PRINCE?

ME? THE MOST DELICIOUS BITE I EVER TOOK?

WE HELD OUR BREATH WAITING FOR DASTAN'S ANSWER. SURELY IN THE KING'S PALACE HE HAD TASTED DELIGHTS BEYOND THE DREAMS OF COMMON SOLDIERS LIKE US.

IT WAS AN APPLE.

AN APPLE FROM THE KING'S ORCHARDS?

NO, IT WAS AN ORDINARY APPLE FROM A STREET STALL IN NASAF... IT WAS BRUISED, TO BOOT.

BUT THAT'S A LONG STORY, FOR ANOTHER TIME.

113

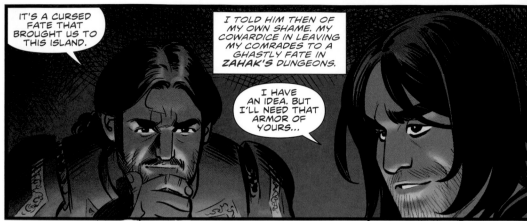

IT'S A CURSED FATE THAT BROUGHT US TO THIS ISLAND.

I TOLD HIM THEN OF MY OWN SHAME. MY COWARDICE IN LEAVING MY COMRADES TO A GHASTLY FATE IN *ZAHAK'S* DUNGEONS.

I HAVE AN IDEA. BUT I'LL NEED THAT ARMOR OF YOURS...

I SOON WISHED I HADN'T.

COME ON, PICK UP YOUR FEET! WE NEED TO GET THERE BEFORE DARK!

OPEN UP-- QUICK! I CAPTURED THESE TWO SINGLE-HANDED FOR *ZAHAK.*

YOU'RE NOT FROM AROUND HERE.

ARE WE GOING TO STAND AROUND TALKING, OR GET THEM TO ZAHAK?

...BECAUSE FROM WHAT I HEARD, HE'S ABOUT TO START EATING HIS OWN GUARDS.

FOLLOW ME.

I KNEW THIS ZAHAK HAD TO BE MONSTROUS. BUT NOT IN MY WORST NIGHTMARES COULD I HAVE IMAGINED WHAT I WAS ABOUT TO SEE.

Ahh...

FINALLY.

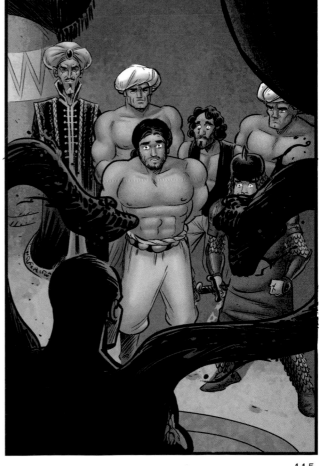

TAKE ME FIRST. I WANT THE HONOR OF SLAKING THE HUNGER OF THE GREAT ZAHAK.

IF ONLY *ALL MY SUBJECTS* SHARED YOUR SENSE OF DUTY.

BRING HIM FORWARD.

KRNCH

LOOK OUT! HE'S LOOSE!

DIE!

DON'T YOU THINK I'VE TRIED THAT?

DON'T YOU THINK I'VE TRIED *EVERYTHING?*

THEY HAVE TO BE FED OR THEY'LL GIVE ME NO PEACE. THERE'S NO OTHER WAY.

THEY *WILL* BE FED.

NO ONE KNOWS... THE BURDENS... OF A KING.

THE PEOPLE BEGGED DASTAN TO STAY AND BE THEIR KING. THE VIZIER OFFERED US HIS OWN DAUGHTERS IN MARRIAGE.. THREE OF THEM, EACH MORE BEAUTIFUL THAN THE NEXT...

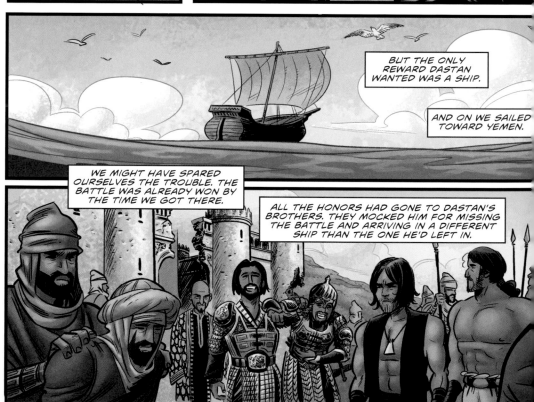

BUT THE ONLY REWARD DASTAN WANTED WAS A SHIP.

AND ON WE SAILED TOWARD YEMEN.

WE MIGHT HAVE SPARED OURSELVES THE TROUBLE. THE BATTLE WAS ALREADY WON BY THE TIME WE GOT THERE.

ALL THE HONORS HAD GONE TO DASTAN'S BROTHERS. THEY MOCKED HIM FOR MISSING THE BATTLE AND ARRIVING IN A DIFFERENT SHIP THAN THE ONE HE'D LEFT IN.

AFTER THEM! DON'T LET THEM GET AWAY!

FOOL-- INCOMPETENT--I LET THEM TALK AND TALK... THE KING WILL HAVE MY HEAD FOR THIS!

...THE ROYAL GUARD...

AND HERE IT COMES.

PRINCE DASTAN HAS RECEIVED YOUR MESSAGE. YOU HAVE TWO MEN AND HIS ROYAL PROPERTY IN YOUR CUSTODY?

YES... WELL... THAT IS...

THE PRINCE ORDERS THAT ON NO CONDITION ARE THESE MEN TO BE HARMED. THEY ARE TO BE SET FREE IMMEDIATELY, WITH HIS APOLOGIES.

YE--YES... OF COURSE! IT'S...IT'S ALREADY BEEN DONE.

I KNEW IN MY BELLY THEY WERE INNOCENT.

Visit www.disneybooks.com
Disney.com/PrinceOfPersia
Printed in the United States of America
First Edition
1 3 5 7 9 10 8 6 4 2

V381-8386-5-10060

Library of Congress Catalog Card Number on file.
ISBN 978-14231-2429-0 (hardcover)
Library of Congress Cataloging-in-Publication Data on file

ISBN 978-14231-2582-2 (paperback)
Library of Congress Catalog Card Number on file